HOLLY KELLER

Angela's
Top-Secret
Computer
Club

Greenwillow Books, New York

The preseparated two-color art was prepared
with a combination of pen-and-ink line
and halftone overlays done in pencil.
The text type is Kuenstler BT.

Library of Congress Cataloging-in-Publication Data
Keller, Holly.
Angela's Top-Secret Computer Club / by Holly Keller.
p.   cm.
Summary: Angela and her friends in the Top-Secret
Computer Club use their knowledge of computers
and email to discover who is causing
all the problems with the school's computer.
ISBN 0-688-15571-5   [1. Computers—Fiction.
2. Schools—Fiction.   3. Mystery and detective stories.]
I. Title.   PZ7.K28132An   1998
[Fic]—dc21   97-6690   CIP   AC

Contents

Angela

Lately I've noticed that things happen to me that almost never happen to anyone else. I am Angela, and even when I don't do anything (at least not anything much) to make them happen, *things* seem to happen to me anyway. My teacher, Mr. Stitch, says that chaos follows me like a shadow, and I guess I know what he means.

The last day of school is a pretty good example. There was a big mess with the report cards that didn't have anything to do with me, but I ended up in the middle of it anyway.

The Top-Secret Computer Club, of which I am a founding member, ended up in the middle of it, too, and that's when it turned into an interesting adventure.

·2·
The Last Day of School

The last day of school began at seven-fifteen when my frequently annoying brother, Ralph, tripped over the sneaker he left in the hall and crashed into my bedroom door. Waking up in the morning isn't the thing I do best, and waking up to a noise like that doesn't make it easier. Harriet, my parakeet, jumped straight up and banged her head on the top of her cage. My puppy, Gus, dove under the bed and skidded into the wall. I heard somewhere that pets and their owners get to be a lot alike, so I guess it's safe to say that Harriet and Gus don't always think Ralph is too cool either.

Ralph has recently announced that he is not "a breakfast person," but he still can't resist coming into the kitchen every morning to share his words of wisdom for the day.

"So, Ange," he said that morning, "are you going to get promoted or are they sending you back to kindergarten?" There was no reason to answer, so I just kept on eating. You might have thought Ralph would get the idea and go away, but no, that wouldn't be like Ralph. "I think I'll probably get an A in English and an A in Math," he said in his most irritating voice. "I heard that Mr. Stitch made up a special grade for you, Angela. . . ."

"RALPH!" Papa shouted from the bathroom. "Aren't you ready to leave yet?"

I gave Ralph the smile that I know he hates (you can see almost all of my teeth), and I went to get dressed.

I LEFT THE HOUSE at ten after eight the way I always do, and I got to school at eight-twenty-five as usual. But the minute I got inside the building, I knew that this was not going to be a normal day. Not even a normal last day. The teachers were buzzing around in the hall like a swarm of mosquitoes, and Mr. Stitch's face was the color of cranberry sauce.

When the bell rang, Mr. Stitch came into the room and practically screamed that everyone should sit down. Mr. Stitch is always upset about something, but this time he was sputtering like the water fountain in the playground that never works. He cleared his throat about ten times and tried to smooth his hair, which was sticking up all over the place.

He finally managed to explain that there was a problem with the report cards and that it would take a little time to straighten it out.

"Instead of talking about our plans for vacation," Mr. Stitch said, "I want everyone to write a short paragraph about what he or she is going to do. I will be in the office. Angela, please be in charge."

Mr. Stitch always picks me for things like that, and I can tell you that it doesn't always feel like the honor Mama says it is. I have to admit that I wasn't very sorry to miss hearing about Frieda's boring trip to her grandmother's house, or the new fishing rod that James was going to use to catch the biggest fish anyone ever saw, but nobody wanted to write a stupid paragraph—and since I was in charge, naturally everybody decided it was my fault.

So I said, "Okay, let's all write something quick, quick, quick, and then we can try to find out what happened to the report cards."

"How?" Amanda asked.

I couldn't really think of anything, so I just said the first thing that came to my mind. "Spies. We'll send out some spies."

There was a big cheer for that, and everybody was happy again. That is, until it was time to do it and nobody wanted to go. So guess who was suddenly a spy? I decided to say that we were all finished with the writing assignment and we didn't know what to do next. That way I could go to the office and pretend I was looking for Mr. Stitch.

James said that I needed to wear a disguise because real spies always did. He gave me his baseball cap, and Peter donated his silver space-camp windbreaker. Amanda lent me her 3-D sunglasses, and I have to admit that I looked pretty good.

There was so much confusion in the office that it took about five minutes before anybody even noticed me. That gave me plenty of time to look around, and I actually saw a few of the messed-up report cards. Incredible. Of course the minute Mr. Stitch laid eyes on me, he sent me speeding back to the classroom. So much for the great disguise. Still, I had seen enough to make a really exciting report.

Most of the normal subjects like history and English had been changed to weird things like "TV Watching" and "Rollerblading." All the grades were C or worse, and everybody was assigned to the wrong class for next year. My report card could have looked like this:

ANGELA SPIEGELHOFF
DAYS ABSENT **5,000**

DAYS TARDY **8,000**

KARATE **F**   ICE FISHING **F**

DOG CATCHING **C**   SCIENCE **D**

TV WATCHING **D**   ROLLERBLADING **C**

PROMOTED TO: **Grade 10**

At first we thought it was pretty funny, but when Mr. Stitch (who almost never finds anything funny anyway) came back to the room, he said this was *really* not funny, because it meant that somebody had figured out how to change everything in the school computer to nonsense. That was impressive.

By the afternoon the grades had been fixed and we were all promoted to the right class, but some of the school's records were lost forever. Of course not everybody was too unhappy about that, like Fred, who was actually pretty glad that his parents couldn't find out how many mornings he had been late.

At lunchtime there were newspaper reporters and TV cameras all over the place. They even came into the cafeteria. Everyone wanted to know what had happened and if anyone had any ideas about who might have done it.

Jake and I were watching one of the TV

men get set up when Ralph came up behind me. "Well, Angela," he said, really loudly so the reporters could hear, "are you the one who did it? Everyone thinks it must have been you."

Sometimes he thinks he's so funny.

But thanks to Ralph, the TV reporter interviewed me right at the beginning of the

story, and that night when we turned on the six o'clock news, there I was! Ralph said he wasn't jealous, but I wouldn't say that he was exactly convincing. Anyway, the reporter kept asking me a lot of questions, and I kept making up a lot of pretty good answers, until for some reason I'll never understand, I told him about the computer club that Isabel, Albert, Jake, and I had recently started. I told him that we really knew a lot about computers and that we could probably solve the whole report-card mystery before the end of summer vacation.

"Really?" he asked.

"Oh, sure," I said to about a zillion people watching the program. "No problem."

And that, of course, was the beginning of the problem.

·3·
T.S.C.C.

About a month ago Mrs. Grover, our school librarian, said she would teach anyone who wanted to learn how to send electronic mail on the computer. Isabel, Jake, Albert, and I all wanted to, and that was how our computer club got started. We got to pick secret passwords for ourselves (mine is Wonder Woman), and then we each got an E-mail address. Mrs. Grover let us choose the name we wanted to use in the address, too. Mine is just **angela@centralschl.com**, but Albert decided he wanted his address to be **einstein@centralschl.com**, which is pretty funny considering how much he hates math.

Anyway, when you turn on the computer you have to enter your E-mail name and your password, and then any messages that were sent to you pop up on the computer screen. It is very cool.

Albert, Isabel, Jake, and I each use a computer in a different part of the library, and we send messages back and forth that nobody else can ever read unless we tell them our passwords, which of course we never will.

Ralph's friend Izzy, who is almost as irritating as Ralph, tried to read my E-mail messages one day by guessing my secret password, but he never even got close.

We can send E-mail to other people in school if we know their addresses, and they can send messages to us, too. Mr. Cook, the science teacher, has a computer in his classroom, and sometimes he sends us messages with science questions. We can also get E-mail from people who are not in school. Albert's mother has a computer in her office, and sometimes she sends us riddles like "What is yellow and lies on its back?" The answer was "A tired school bus," but nobody got it.

Even though school is over for the year, some kids always stay around during the summer to help out in the office or to work on special stuff, and Mrs. Grover said we could keep having our computer club meetings in the library until she went away on vacation. So the day after the big report-card mess we all showed up in the library, and right away Mrs. Grover wanted to know exactly how we thought we were going to solve the mystery.

Naturally everybody looked at me. And naturally I didn't have a clue.

"I don't think we should talk about it yet," I said, and I tried to sound like I really had a plan.

Jake was furious, because he said that about a thousand kids had called him the night before to ask what the club was going to do, and he had known I was just making it up, as usual. Some people have no imagination.

Well, anyway, we went to our computers, and I entered my password so that I could get my messages. There was one from Mr. Cook that said "Have a very wonderful summer vacation" and another from Isabel asking whether I thought Mrs. Grover had a long nose. "Yes," I wrote back, because not even Mrs. Grover can read what I write without knowing my secret password.

I was in the middle of writing to Jake when Albert called out, "Wow, look at this!" and we all went over to look. There was a message on Albert's screen that none of us had written. It was sent to Albert's e-mail address — **einstein@centralschl.com**, and it was signed "Black Cat." Albert had no idea who that could be.

One of the things about E-mail is that the computer address of the person who sends you a message is printed on the screen along with the message. So we knew right away that it wasn't from Albert's mother. The message said:

Full speed ahead
Repeat same program
—Black Cat

The address of the person who sent it was **blackcat@xyz.com**.

"I don't like the sound of it," Isabel said.

Jake thought it was probably just somebody fooling around, but I was pretty excited.

I couldn't help hoping that it might be something that would help the computer club solve the report-card mystery before school started again.

Mrs. Grover was about ready to close the library for the day, so we decided to print out a copy of the message and talk about it later.

Albert wrote "Top Secret" at the top of the page, and we agreed not to mention it to anyone.

I said we could move the meeting to my house as long as Ralph wasn't home. Luckily he was over at Izzy's, so the coast was clear. Jake made a KEEP OUT sign to tape onto the outside of my bedroom door. I thought it would probably be a good idea to cover Harriet's cage, so she would think it was night and go to sleep. Sometimes she repeats things that you definitely wish she wouldn't.

ANYHOW, THAT'S HOW the computer club became the Top-Secret Computer Club. We used my new markers to make our membership cards. The letters *T.S.C.C.* were red with black outlines. Albert became Agent Number One, I was Agent Number Two, Jake was Agent Number Three, and Isabel was Agent Number Four.

I thought we should have a special code word so that if one of us wanted to call a meeting or something, he or she could just say the word and the rest of us would know what it meant. Everybody liked the idea, even though it took us about all day to agree on what the word should be. We finally chose "mercury," because Mr. Stitch had told us that Mercury was a speedy messenger. The idea was that one of us could just call the others, say "mercury," and hang up. We would all know that there was a problem and that we needed to meet, but nobody else would know what we were talking about.

Of course the first time Jake called and said "mercury," he blurted it out before he realized that it was Ralph who had answered the phone. Then instead of hanging up, he asked Ralph if he could speak to Agent Number Two, and that was pretty much the end of that one. Once Ralph gets hold of something he thinks is a secret, he's a worse pain than ever. He started calling me Agent Number Two no matter where we were until I threatened to flush his tropical fish down the toilet. Luckily he got bored after a while and forgot about it. But the club had to forget about it, too.

PROBABLY THE WHOLE THING would have been forgotten except that a couple of weeks later Albert got a second E-mail message from "Black Cat." It was even stranger than the first:

If possible
Delete everything
—Black Cat

Naturally we didn't have any idea what this one meant either. Jake thought that we should send a message back to this Black Cat person and see if we could find out who he was, but I just had a feeling that we should wait. "Wait for what?" Jake wanted to know, and I wasn't really sure. It was just a feeling.

By then it was the beginning of July, and the Top-Secret Computer Club had come up with absolutely nothing.

New Ideas

The club had an emergency meeting to decide what to do next. Isabel made a list of the things we knew. It was pretty short because we only knew three things:

1) Someone had broken into the school computer and messed up all the report cards.

2) Someone named Black Cat was sending strange messages to Albert that might be related to the report-card incident. (Jake insisted on using the word "incident" because

he watches a lot of detective stories on TV.)

3) One of us had told the world that our computer club was going to solve the mystery before school started again. (Naturally we couldn't leave that out.)

I decided it was a good time to announce my latest idea.

"What if someone is sending these messages to our Albert thinking that **einstein@centralschl.com** is somebody else's E-mail address? Since no two people can have the same E-mail address, Albert is getting the messages by mistake. Maybe for some reason Black Cat thinks that the person he wants to reach uses the name Einstein in his E-mail address, but he doesn't. He uses a different name, and Black Cat just doesn't know it."

Jake and Isabel didn't think that was very likely, but then I got to the really good part. "Even if Black Cat is using the wrong name, the second part of the address might be right, and that means that the *other* person would be using a school computer. In other words, the 'Einstein' that Black Cat is trying to reach is probably someone in this school. In fact, he could be here at this very minute."

All of a sudden everyone was listening.

"You mean he could be someone we know?" Isabel asked.

"Maybe it's the principal," Jake said, but nobody thought that was really too funny.

We wrote a list of the things we still needed to know:

1) Who is Black Cat?

2) What do the two messages mean, and are they really related to the report-card incident?

3) Is there somebody else called Einstein?

4) Is the other Einstein using a school computer?

Jake thought we should start by checking out all the other computers in the school, so we each chose a different part of the building to investigate. There were a few teachers working in classrooms and a few people in the office, but a lot of doors were locked. It felt pretty creepy to be walking around in the empty halls. When Mr. Biggs, the janitor, suddenly appeared out of nowhere, I was so scared it felt like my hair was standing straight up on my head.

"Well, hello, Angela," he said. "What are you doing up here?"

"Oh, nothing much," I answered, trying to sound pretty casual and hoping that my hair was really normal. "Just looking around."

"There's hardly anybody here today," he said. "Are you looking for something in particular?"

I told him that I was on a computer search, which must have sounded pretty ridiculous, and he said the only one he knew of was in the biology room. I told him that if it was okay, I would just stroll down and have a look. Which I did.

When the club met back in the library, we had found a total of thirteen computers. Five were right there in the library and four were in the office. There was one in Mr. Cook's room and two in the math room, but they were all locked up. Number thirteen was the one in the biology room, and we decided that had to be it.

Jake said that detective stories always have a "stakeout" and that we needed to stake out computer number thirteen to see who was using it. And then of course everyone looked at me.

"It has to be you," Isabel said, "because you're the only one with spying experience."

Right.

THE FIRST TIME, I was so nervous my knees felt like Jell-O, but I actually got to be pretty good at knowing when I could sneak down the hall without meeting Mr. Biggs. The only problem was that whenever I went to check, nobody was using the computer. Jake said that sometimes a stakeout lasted for weeks.

Then finally, on the third day, when I was just about to give up, Mrs. Grover sent me down to the office to get something for her. A kid named Sammy was working on one of the computers. I asked him some questions about what he was doing, and he just kept saying a lot of dumb things like "figuring out how many times the cafeteria served mashed potatoes for lunch." I thought that sounded really suspicious.

Since I wasn't having any luck upstairs, I decided to move my stakeout to the office. The only problem was that it was hard not to

attract attention when I kept showing up every half hour. Jake thought I should try another disguise, but seeing how much luck I had had with the first one, it was hard to get too excited about that idea.

Anyhow, all I found out was that mashed potatoes were served thirty-eight times and green beans twenty-six times, and that most kids ate peanut butter and jelly. I finally asked Sammy straight out if he had seen any black cats around lately, and he looked at me like I was from the moon. I guess he was just counting mashed potatoes.

I MADE ONE LAST CHECK in the biology room on my way back to the library, and when I looked in the door, my heart almost stopped. An older girl named Margaret, and who else but Ralph's pain-in-the-neck friend Izzy, were actually in there. They were measuring earthworms or something. Izzy was taking the measurements and Margaret was entering them into the computer.

"It's a summer project," Margaret said.

"Yeah," said Izzy. "Miss Einstein here is the computer brain. I just measure the worms, and she does all the rest."

Suddenly my scalp started to feel like a cactus.

"Do you always call her Miss Einstein?" I asked, even though I knew Izzy would tell

Ralph that I was hanging around and asking dumb questions.

"Yup," Izzy said. "Me and everybody else."

Margaret got really mad and bopped Izzy on the head with her notebook.

"But not for much longer," she said, sort of mysteriously.

Izzy tried to drop an earthworm down the back of Margaret's dress, but I didn't wait around to see what happened.

It took me about three seconds to run downstairs. I crashed smack into Albert and almost killed him, but I was too excited to stop. I told everybody about Izzy calling Margaret "Miss Einstein," and then it came to me in a flash—I had been right all along. Someone really was sending E-mail messages to Margaret thinking her address was **einstein@centralschl.com**. Probably the right address was **margaret@centralschl.com**, or at

least something like that. Since Albert's address was **einstein@centralschl.com**, he was getting those weird messages that were really meant for Margaret.

"Brilliant," Albert said, and actually, I thought so, too.

The next day I decided that it was time to have a little talk with Margaret. When I went back to the biology room, she was working at the computer again, but this time Izzy wasn't there. Margaret seemed to be searching for something, and she looked really upset.

"I just can't understand it," she said. "I'm expecting a message from someone, and I have no idea why I can't find it."

"Why don't you write to him?" I asked, since that seemed pretty logical.

"I can't," Margaret answered, "because I don't know who it is yet. It's a friend of my brother, Billy."

"So why don't you just ask Billy?" I said.

"Because Billy is at Boy Scout camp for the summer," Margaret said angrily. "Anyway, Billy is such a brat that he probably wouldn't tell me. He thinks he's so great just because he's popular and everyone does what he says."

"I think it's funny that you're called Miss Einstein," I said, even though I knew I was on really dangerous ground.

"Well, I don't," Margaret snapped. "And if Billy keeps his promise, I won't be after school starts again."

I was just about to ask her what she meant when Izzy came along. They started to work on their earthworms again, and I left.

Well, you might have thought that after all that hard work the club would have been pretty excited, but nobody seemed very worked up.

"We still don't know why Black Cat is sending her those messages," Isabel pointed out.

"Or," Jake added, "what they mean or what we should do next."

"Or," Albert said, "if you don't mind my pointing out a pretty big problem, whether this has anything at all to do with the report cards."

It seemed to me that it was finally time to send Black Cat an E-mail message and see if we could find out something about him. At least everyone agreed about that. I figured we should send the message Margaret would send if she knew where to send it.

"Right," Jake said. "Albert can write 'Dear Black Cat, why haven't you sent any messages?' and he can sign it 'Einstein.' Since Black Cat will still send it back to **einstein@centralschl.com**, Albert will get the answer."

Things were really getting exciting now. Albert typed the message on his computer and sent it to **blackcat@xyz.com**. Then there was nothing to do but wait. Naturally Mrs. Grover decided that she needed to close the library for the day so that she could buy groceries. We agreed to meet at nine o'clock the next morning.

The good news was that in the morning there was an answer from Black Cat:

I sent two messages—no idea where they went. Here they are again:
Full speed ahead
Repeat same program
If possible
Delete everything
—Black Cat

The bad news was that we still didn't have a clue about who this Black Cat person was, and Mrs. Grover announced that she was going on vacation.

·5·
Some Surprises

So all of a sudden half the summer was over and the library was closing. The Top-Secret Computer Club decided that it needed to work really fast if it was going to figure anything out by September. I pointed out that nothing was ever going to happen unless Margaret got her messages.

We knew that we couldn't forward Black Cat's messages to Margaret by E-mail, because she would be able to see that they didn't really come from Black Cat. Albert thought we should just type them out and leave them taped to Margaret's computer.

"Sure," Jake said. "We could write a note from Black Cat saying that he suspected Margaret's computer was bugged and that she wasn't getting all her E-mail messages. Which is almost half true."

"Right," Albert added. "And that's why Black Cat arranged to have someone deliver them to her."

It was sort of a wild idea, but nobody was exactly coming up with anything better. So Albert copied the messages, and Jake wrote a note to go with them, and (big surprise here) everyone agreed that I was the logical one to make the delivery.

The next morning I went to the biology room as early as I could. There was no trace of Mr. Biggs in the hall, so I just sort of slithered along the wall until I reached the right door. I peeked inside. There was nobody there.

It only took a minute to tape the note and the messages onto Margaret's computer screen, but my stomach felt like someone had dropped a whole grapefruit into it. Then just as I started to leave, I heard Izzy's voice. I ran behind the door to hide, and it occurred to me that I might finally find out what it feels like to faint.

Izzy came into the room, and Margaret was with him. Luckily they went right into the storage closet to get the worms, and that's when I slipped out. I told the club that I was NEVER going to do that again. And I meant it.

So now the right Einstein had the messages from Black Cat, whoever he was, and we didn't know what else to do. I was going to spend the month of August at Camp Wabonka-in-the-Hills, and Jake and Isabel were going away, too, so we couldn't really do anything very much anyway.

We decided to meet again the week before school started.

I HAD A REALLY GREAT TIME at camp. I learned how to mount butterflies, and Mama said my collection was so pretty she was going to have it framed. But by the end of the month I could hardly wait to get home to work on the report-card mystery. The library was open again, and the T.S.C.C. was back in action.

I thought it was time to lay a trap for Black Cat and find out who he was. All we had to do was send Black Cat an E-mail message from Einstein (which Black Cat would think was from Margaret) and ask him to meet Einstein someplace. Then we could deliver another message to Margaret from Black Cat telling her to meet him in the same place. Naturally we would hide nearby and see who he was.

But Jake pointed out that when Margaret and Black Cat met, they would realize in about three seconds that they hadn't sent the messages to each other.

"Then," Isabel said, "they will figure out that there really was someone else getting the messages Black Cat was trying to send to Margaret."

"And," Jake added, "once Black Cat has

Margaret's real E-mail address, Albert won't get any more of the messages meant for Margaret, and we will never find out anything."

I had to admit that Isabel and Jake had a point, but the first day of school was only a week away and we weren't exactly making amazing progress.

Everything changed that afternoon when Albert got another E-mail message from Black Cat.

This one was even more discouraging.

After this message
Your instructions are complete
—Black Cat

The club had another urgent meeting. This time Jake had to sneak into the biology room and tape the new message to Margaret's computer. He said he wasn't scared at all, but I wouldn't say that everyone believed him.

Anyway, we decided to copy all the messages onto the blackboard in the same order we had gotten them, and that's when we made the next big discovery. Putting together the first letters of each message definitely spelled the word "Friday," and we knew that couldn't be an accident.

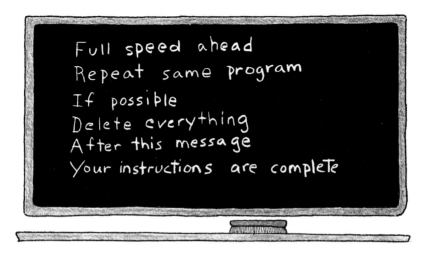

Full speed ahead
Repeat same program
If possible
Delete everything
After this message
Your instructions are complete

For a minute nobody could say anything. Finding a major clue like that was almost as scary as not finding one.

"Now what are we going to do?" Isabel asked. "We have no idea *what* is going to happen on Friday, since we don't understand what any of the messages mean."

"Well," I said, "I guess we could just wait and see." And that was more or less what we did.

·6·
Friday

The Friday before the opening of school finally came, and by lunchtime it looked as if absolutely nothing was going to happen. I figured that just when the Top-Secret Computer Club seemed to be about to solve the mystery, the whole thing might turn into a big fizzle.

Then, at about one o'clock, Jake called with the incredible news that his mother had met Mr. Cook in the drugstore, and he had told her that there was another terrible mess at school.

"Worse than the report-card thing!" Jake shouted into the phone. "It's the schedules this time. The office was getting them ready for Monday, and all of a sudden the school computer went wacko. All the class meeting times and places were completely erased!"

Well, it didn't exactly take a genius to figure it out now. Margaret, or "Miss Einstein the computer brain," was the one who was making the computers act crazy, and Black Cat was telling her what to do and when to do it.

"Full speed ahead / Repeat same program" must have meant that Margaret was supposed to mess up the schedules the same way she had messed up the report cards. Since the messages didn't mention the schedules, she must have already known that.

"If possible / Delete everything" was exactly

what had happened when all the class times and meeting places disappeared from the computer. Since the last message told Margaret when to do it, her instructions were complete because she didn't need any more. WOW!

Albert, Isabel, Jake, and I went tearing over to school. Mrs. Nettle, the principal, was shaking all over. Mr. Stitch was there, too, and he was even more cranberry-sauce colored than on the last day of school. We tried to get them to listen to our story, but it wasn't easy. It probably didn't help that we were all talking at once. Finally I stood up on a chair and whistled, which actually got everyone's attention.

"We already know one of the people who is doing this," I said. "The other person is using the name Black Cat, and we can find out who that is if you will just let us into the

library to use a computer. But you can't tell anybody *anything* yet."

Mr. Stitch could hardly speak. "Angela," he sputtered, "if this is another one of your ridiculous schemes . . ."

But Mrs. Grover was already on her way to the library.

Albert sat down at his computer and sent the following message to Black Cat:

The job is done but I have to see you right away.
Meet me at four o'clock in front of the post office.
—Einstein

By four o'clock we were all feeling as if we had butterflies inside. Me especially. We waited near (but not too near) the post office to see who was going to come along. Mrs. Grover was inside the building, watching through the window.

At about two minutes after four, Jimmy Black and Catherine Moss strolled up to the post office and stopped. They looked around a few times, and then they just waited.

We didn't pay too much attention to them

at first because we weren't really expecting two people. But when nobody else showed up, we began to wonder.

"That's him!" Albert whispered. "I mean them. It's gotta be."

"No," Isabel said. "Margaret only talked about one person, not two."

"But she never met Black Cat," I whispered back, "so maybe she doesn't know."

Anyway, Jimmy and Catherine waited about ten minutes, and then they left.

Mrs. Grover came running out of the post office and said "Congratulations!" but we weren't exactly sure what she meant. Then she showed us a paper on which she had written the names Jimmy BLACK and CATherine Moss, and there it was. Black Cat!

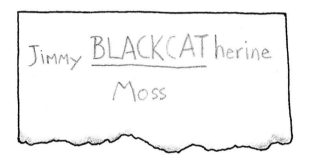

We just stood there sort of dazed until Mrs. Grover said we had to hurry back to school that instant. Then of course we had to tell everyone the whole story again, especially the part about Margaret and the E-mail messages.

Margaret, Jimmy, and Catherine (and their parents) got called to school. I told Mrs. Nettle that it would probably be a good idea to call Margaret's brother, Billy, too. Then Mrs. Nettle said her head was throbbing and would the Top-Secret Computer Club mind waiting in the hall.

Boy, were we mad! Things were finally getting interesting, and we definitely didn't want to miss any of it. We decided to go into the teachers' coat room, which was right next door to Mrs. Nettle's office, because we knew that we would be able to hear pretty well in there. Of course Jake was making such a big deal about tiptoeing around and not making any noise that he tripped over the waste-paper basket, but I guess Mrs. Nettle was too upset to pay any attention to it.

Anyhow, we didn't get to hear very much because Margaret, Jimmy, and Catherine didn't really say very much. That is, until Billy got there.

Margaret started shouting at him the minute he walked in the door. "It's all your fault!" she yelled.

"No, it isn't," Billy shouted back. "You were the one who was bragging that you had figured out how to change stuff in the school computer, and all I said was that I bet you couldn't."

"And I said I would prove it," Margaret said

to Mrs. Nettle, "if he made sure that everyone stopped calling me 'Miss Einstein the computer brain,' and he promised. Then after I changed all the report cards, Billy said I still had to do one more thing. 'It will have something to do with the schedules,' he told me, but he didn't know exactly what. Somebody called Black Cat was supposed to send me an E-mail message telling me what to do and when to do it."

Mrs. Nettle asked Billy why he had wanted to mess up the schedules.

Suddenly Billy didn't sound so sure of himself. "I found out that I was going to be in Mrs. Brady's math class, and I had to get out of it. Mrs. Brady hates me because one day in the cafeteria I tossed half of my sandwich to Charlie Harris and it accidentally hit her in the back. There was mustard all over her dress, and she told me I had better not ever cross her path again. And there I was assigned to her class. After I saw that Margaret really could break into the school computer, I figured that if she erased all the schedules and they had to be written all over again, I might have a chance of ending up with a different teacher."

Mrs. Nettle groaned.

Well, the Top-Secret Computer Club was feeling pretty good. Isabel whispered that we should probably get out of the coat room before someone came looking for us, so we slipped back into the hall one by one.

Jake and Albert wanted to know how I had figured out that Billy was really behind it all.

"No problem," I said in my best detective voice. "I didn't really know that it was Billy who got Margaret to break into the computer the first time, or what he had promised her, but Margaret told me herself that the E-mail

message she was waiting for was coming from a friend of Billy's.

"She also said that Billy was away at Boy Scout camp for the summer, and that seemed pretty suspicious. Anybody who thought about it would know that breaking into the computer a second time would make it much easier to be caught, but Billy knew that he was going to be away so he couldn't be blamed for the messages.

"He told Jimmy and Catherine to tell Margaret what to do, but they didn't want to be caught either, so they decided to call themselves Black Cat to make sure that Margaret didn't know who they were. I just figured that if Billy was helping to plan the second break-in, he must have been in on the first one, too."

I have to admit that everyone was pretty amazed.

We heard that Billy, Catherine, and Jimmy got about a zillion hours of detention, and Billy still had to be in Mrs. Brady's class. Since Margaret was the only one who knew how to unscramble the schedules, Mrs. Nettle made her spend the whole weekend at school doing it. But Mrs. Nettle also had a serious talk with Billy, and he promised to tell everyone to stop calling Margaret names.

Mrs. Grover told us that it was because of the Top-Secret Computer Club's good detective work that the first day of school was pretty much a normal first day. The big exception was that by lunchtime everyone knew who had solved the mystery.

I don't think I ever want to be a detective again, but being famous wasn't too bad. Isabel, Albert, and Jake didn't seem to mind too much either. Even Ralph had to admit that we had done a good job.

The newspaper and TV reporters came back and did a whole story about the Top-Secret Computer Club. They all wanted to know what we were going to do next, but this

time I decided not to make any great promises.

The club still meets in the library twice a week, of course, and if you want to, you can always send me an E-mail message at **angela@centralschl.com**.